The Black Cat

ALLAN AHLBERG · ANDRE AMSTUTZ

HEINEMANN · LONDON

William Heinemann Ltd
Michelin House
81 Fulham Road, London SW3 6RB
LONDON · MELBOURNE · AUCKLAND
First published 1990
Text copyright © Allan Ahlberg 1990
Illustrations copyright © André Amstutz 1990
The right of Allan Ahlberg and André Amstutz to be identified as
author and illustrator of this work has been asserted by them in
accordance with the Copyright, Designs and Patents Act 1988
ISBN 434 92499 7
Printed in Great Britain by
Cambus Litho, East Kilbride

In a dark dark town,
on a cold cold night,
under a starry starry sky,
down a slippery slippery slope,
on a bumpety bumpety sledge . . .

a little skeleton is sliding . . .
and sliding . . .
and crashing – wallop!

The little skeleton
loses a leg in the snow.
A white leg in snow
is hard to find.
A black cat in snow
is easy to find.
What is <u>she</u> doing here?

The little skeleton and the big skeleton
go to the bone-yard
to get a new leg
for the little skeleton.

They play around with the bones
for a while . . .
and go home to bed.

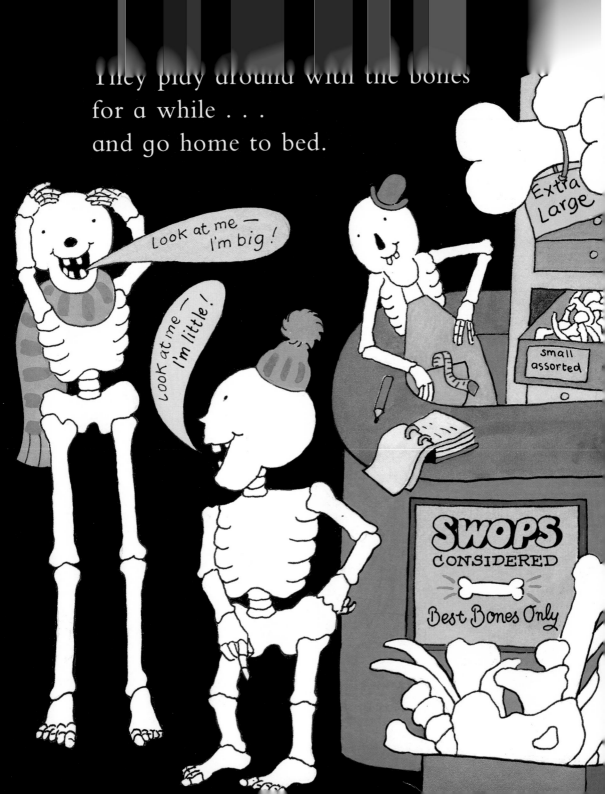

Then . . .
in the dark dark town,
on <u>another</u> cold cold night,
under a starry starry sky,
down a slippery slippery slope,
on a bumpety bumpety sledge . . .

two skeletons are sliding . . .
and sliding . . .
and sliding . . .
and crashing – bang!
WALLOP!
This time the big skeleton
loses a leg in the snow.

A white leg in snow
is hard to find.
A black cat is easy.
Is she still here?
I wonder why.

The big skeleton
and the little skeleton
go to the bone-yard
to get a new leg
for the big skeleton.

They play around again with the bones
and go home to bed.

Then . . .
in the dark town,
on the <u>next</u> night,
under a starry sky,
with a moon, too,
down a slippery slope,
in the frosty air,
on a bumpety sledge . . .

<u>three</u> skeletons are sliding . . .
and sliding . . .
and shouting . . .
and barking!
And banging! Wallop!

CRASH!

This time the big skeleton
and the little skeleton
lose the dog skeleton.
A white dog in snow
is hard to find.
But a noisy dog is easy to find.
So is a black cat!

woof!

The dog skeleton chases the cat.
Now we know —
that's what she is here for!

The dog chases the cat
up and down
the dark dark hill,
in and out
of the dark dark bone-yard,

round and round
the dark dark streets
and down and down
to the dark dark cellar.

But a black cat in a cellar
is very hard to find.
Can <u>you</u> see her?

Well, the dog skeleton couldn't,
and the little skeleton couldn't,
and the big skeleton didn't even try.
So off they went – at last – to bed.

Meanwhile . . .
in the same town,
on the same night,
under the same sky,
down the same slope,
a bumpety sledge is sliding . . .

with a black cat on it.

The End